COYOTE TALES

COYOTE TALES

·

Thomas King

ILLUSTRATIONS BY
Byron Eggenschwiler

GROUNDWOOD BOOKS
HOUSE OF ANANSI PRESS
TORONTO   BERKELEY

Groundwood Books / House of Anansi Press
groundwoodbooks.com

We acknowledge for their financial support of our publishing program the
Canada Council for the Arts, the Ontario Arts Council and the Government of
Canada.

 Canada Council Conseil des Arts
for the Arts du Canada

ONTARIO ARTS COUNCIL
CONSEIL DES ARTS DE L'ONTARIO
an Ontario government agency
un organisme du gouvernement de l'Ontario

With the participation of the Government of Canada
Avec la participation du gouvernement du Canada | **Canadä**

Library and Archives Canada Cataloguing in Publication
King, Thomas, author
Coyote tales / Thomas King ; pictures by Byron Eggenschwiler.
Contents: Coyote's new suit — Coyote sings to the moon.
Issued in print and electronic formats.
ISBN 978-1-55498-833-4 (bound). — ISBN 978-1-55498-835-8 (html). —
ISBN 978-1-55498-836-5 (mobi)
I. Eggenschwiler, Byron, illustrator II. King, Thomas.
Coyote's new suit. III. King, Thomas. Coyote sings to the moon. IV. Title.
PS8571.I5298C698 2017   jC813'.54   C2015-908456-3
C2015-908457-1

Jacket illustration by Byron Eggenschwiler
Design by Michael Solomon

Groundwood Books is committed to protecting our natural environment. As
part of our efforts, the interior of this book is printed on paper that contains
100% post-consumer recycled fibers, is acid-free and is processed chlorine-free.

Printed and bound in Canada

MIX
Paper from
responsible sources
FSC® C016245

CONTENTS

COYOTE SINGS
TO THE MOON

*For Elizabeth and Benjamin,
who think Coyote's singing
got a bum rap — TK*

A long time ago, before animals stopped talking to human beings, Old Woman lived in the woods by a pond. And every evening, she walked down to the pond and waited for the moon to come up.

In those days, the moon was much closer to the earth, and the light from the moon was much brighter. And when the full moon rose above the trees, Old Woman sang out in a strong voice, "Moon, Moon, Full Moon."

And when the moon was a half moon, she sang, "Moon, Moon, Half Moon."

And when it was a crescent, she sang, "Moon, Moon, Crescent Moon."

One evening, all the animals in the woods went down to the pond just to hear Old Woman sing to the moon.

"What a beautiful voice," said the moose.

"Yes," said the ducks. "But we need a livelier beat."

"And a little cool percussion," said the beavers, ba-dopity-bop-bopping their tails on the water.

"Doo-wop, doo-wop," said the turtles and the frogs. "Don't forget the harmony."

So, one by one, all the animals joined in with Old Woman and sang to the moon.

"Moon, Moon, Full Moon."

One evening, Coyote heard Old Woman and the animals singing to the moon.

"Pardon me," said Coyote, smiling his Coyote smile. "Exactly what are you doing?"

"We're singing to the moon," said Old Woman.

"Well," said Coyote, taking out his comb and brushing his coat, checking his teeth with his tongue and wiping his nose on his arm. "What you need is a good tenor."

"No! No!" shouted all the animals. "You have a terrible singing voice!"

"Yes," said Old Woman. "Your voice could scare Moon away."

"Hummph," said Coyote, whose feelings were hurt. "Why would anyone want to sing to Moon, anyway?"

"Moon is our friend," said Old Woman. "She travels all over the world just so we can have light at night."

"Who wants light at night?" said Coyote. "That silly Moon is so bright, I can hardly sleep. Why, I wouldn't sing with you if you begged me."

•

Now, Moon heard Coyote, and the more she listened, the angrier she got.

"Okay," she said to herself. "Let's see how Coyote likes it dark." And she packed her bags, slid out of the sky and dove down into the pond.

When Moon dove into the pond, the whole world got really bright.

"Hey!" said Coyote. "How come it's so bright?"

And then it got really dark.

"Hey!" said Coyote. "How come it's so dark?"

And when Old Woman and Coyote stopped arguing to catch their breath and they looked up in the sky, they saw that Moon was gone.

"This is your fault," said Old Woman. "Moon must have heard your bad thoughts."

"Well," said Coyote, "at least now I can get some sleep."

As soon as Coyote left, Old Woman called the animals together.

"We have to find Moon and get her to go back into the sky," said Old Woman, "or this world is going to be messed up."

"But where would Moon go?" said Moose.

"I don't know," said Old Woman. "But we better start looking."

So all the animals and Old Woman began searching through the dark for Moon.

•

While the animals and Old Woman were searching, Coyote was trying to find his way home.

"I think it's in this direction," said Coyote, and he walked into a tree.

"Hey!" said Tree. "Watch where you're going."

"Sorry," said Coyote. "But it's dark."

"That's because some fur-brain insulted Moon," said Tree, "and she has gone away."

"I can see just fine," said Coyote, and he walked into a large boulder.

"I'll bet that hurt," said Boulder.

"Ouch," said Coyote. "I'm trying to find my way home."

"Sure could use a little moonlight," said Boulder.

"Never mind," said Coyote.

Coyote tried to feel his way in the dark, but he kept bumping into trees and rocks and slipping on wet moss and tripping over sneaky roots.

"Maybe I should just sleep here tonight," said Coyote, "and go home in the morning."

Coyote felt around and found a nice flat spot, and he felt around some more and found something soft and warm.

"This will make a cozy pillow," said Coyote, as he fluffed up the soft and warm thing and put it under his head.

Just as Coyote was falling asleep, the pillow began to move.

"Stop that," said Coyote. "I'm trying to sleep."

"So am I," said the pillow.

Coyote couldn't see a thing, but his nose told him that he may have made a big mistake. Coyote sniffed a little here and he sniffed a little there.

"I hope you're a cuddly sack of garbage," said Coyote.

"Try again," said the pillow.

"A warm pile of moose poop?"

"Nope."

"A skunk?" said Coyote.

"Right!" said Skunk, and he sprayed Coyote all over with really bad-smelling skunk business.

"EEEEYOOOOW!" yelled Coyote, and he jumped up and ran off as fast as he could. He ran and ran and ran and ran.

And ran right off a cliff.

"Oops!" said Coyote. "I can't watch ..." And Coyote closed his eyes and held onto his tail as he fell and fell and fell.

And fell right into the pond.

•

In the meantime, Old Woman and the animals were still looking for Moon.

But they couldn't find her.

"Did you look in that old hollow tree?" said Old Woman.

"We looked there," said the squirrels.

"Did you look in the cave?"

"Yes," said the bears. "We looked there, too."

"Maybe she's hiding behind the waterfall," said Old Woman.

"No," said the deer. "She's not there."

Old Woman sat down on a rock and put her head in her hand.

"Now, where could that Moon be?"

•

When Coyote opened his eyes, he was at the bottom of the pond.

"Oh dear," said Coyote. "This is embarrassing."

Then he noticed something curious. Instead of being cold and dark at the bottom of the pond, it was nice and bright.

"Hmmmm," said Coyote. "This is very curious."

Coyote walked along the bottom of the pond a little ways, and there, lying on a beach blanket under a beach umbrella, playing chess with a sunfish, was Moon.

"There you are," cried Coyote.

"Go away," said Moon. "I've almost won this game."

"Checkmate!" said Sunfish, taking Moon's

knight with his bishop. "Good grief, what stinks?"

"Never mind," said Coyote.

"Let's play again," said Moon, wrinkling her nose. "Phew, what stinks?"

"Never mind," said Coyote. "You have to get back up in the sky."

"I like it here," said Moon.

"But you have to get back up in the sky," said Coyote.

"Have you noticed that you're underwater?" said Moon.

"Oh boy," Coyote thought to himself. "I better get some help. I better get some air!"

•

Old Woman and all the animals were sitting at the edge of the pond, feeling glum, when Coyote popped out of the water.

"You again!" said Old Woman.

"Relax," said Coyote. "I've found Moon. She's at the bottom of the pond."

Old Woman and all the animals put their heads into the pond, and sure enough, there was Moon playing chess with Sunfish.

"This is a fine mess you've made," Old Woman told Coyote. "Now what are we going to do?"

So Coyote and the animals and Old Woman sat on the grass by the pond in the dark and thought.

After a while, Old Woman stood up.

"All right," she said. "First, we have to build a raft."

So all of the next day, when they could see what they were doing, Old Woman and the animals and Coyote built a raft. And just before the sun disappeared, everybody got on the raft and floated out to where Moon was lounging on the bottom of the pond.

"All right," said Old Woman. "Everybody sing. Everybody, that is, except Coyote."

"That's not very nice," said Coyote. "After all, I found Moon."

"Just sit there and be quiet," said Old Woman.

Old Woman began to sing first.

"Moon, Moon, come back soon."

And then, one by one, all the animals joined in.

"Moon, Moon, come back soon."

They sang for hours and hours.

"Moon, Moon, come back soon."

But nothing happened. And when Old Woman looked underwater, Moon was still playing chess and relaxing on the beach blanket under the beach umbrella.

"Okay," said Old Woman. "Now we get serious."

Old Woman moved all the animals off to one side of the raft.

"Stop singing," she said, "and cover your ears."

"Okay," said all the animals.

Old Woman tried to smile at Coyote.

"I was wrong about your singing," she said. "You have a beautiful voice, and I think if you sing all by yourself, Moon will go back up in the sky."

"A solo?" said Coyote, trying to keep his tongue from falling out of his head.

"But you have to sing really loud," said Old Woman.

"I'll sing really, really loud," said Coyote.

"But," said Old Woman, "don't sing until I give you the signal."

Coyote took out his comb and brushed his coat. He ran his tongue over his teeth and wiped his nose on his arm.

Old Woman sat on the raft with the animals and covered her ears.

"Okay," she said, closing her eyes. "Hit it."

Coyote stood up straight, pointed his nose at the stars, opened his mouth and began to sing.

"YEEOO-EEEOOO-WAAAAH-YOOOO-OOO!"

"Yikes!" screamed Old Woman and all the animals.

"YOOOO-EEEEEYOOOOOOOW-YOO-OWWWWW!" sang Coyote.

"Stop! Stop!" screamed Old Woman and all the animals. "It's worse than we thought."

But Coyote didn't hear them. He kept right on singing.

Down at the bottom of the pond, Moon was just about to take Sunfish's queen with her rook when she heard Coyote.

"What is that awful noise?" said Moon.

"It's a good thing I don't have ears," said Sunfish.

Coyote's singing got louder and louder. Moon put her fingers in her ears, but it didn't help.

"Who is making that horrible noise?" said Moon, and she packed up her umbrella and her blanket and swam to the top of the pond to see what was happening.

When Old Woman saw Moon coming to the surface, she yelled at Coyote, "Sing louder!"

Just as Moon came out of the water and looked around, Coyote took a deep breath and sang as loud as he could.

"AAAAWOOOOOOO, AAAWOOOOOOOO-OOOOOO!"

"AAAGGGGGGH!" screamed Moon, and she leapt up into the sky.

"AAAWWWOOOOOO,"sang Coyote. "EEEE-YOOOOOOOOWW!"

Moon climbed into the sky as fast as she could, trying to get away from Coyote's singing.

"Enough!" yelled Old Woman.

But Coyote didn't hear her, and he kept on singing, and Moon kept on climbing.

Old Woman could see that if she didn't shut Coyote up, Moon would climb into the sky until she disappeared. So, quick as she could, Old Woman grabbed Coyote's tongue and wrapped it around his mouth so he couldn't sing anymore.

But Coyote's tongue was long and slippery, and by the time she had Coyote's mouth all wrapped, Moon was much farther away than

before and the light from Moon was very dim.

"Oh dear," said Old Woman. "This didn't exactly work out the way I planned."

"Wouya pwease umwapp ma tongue," said Coyote, with his tongue wrapped around his mouth.

"But I guess it will have to do," said Old Woman.

"Anything to keep Coyote from singing," said the animals.

But just then, Moon began sneaking out of the sky toward that pond.

"Look out, look out!" all the animals yelled to Old Woman. "Moon is sneaking out of the sky."

Old Woman looked up. Moon was picking up speed, heading for that pond. Old Woman grabbed Coyote's tongue and unwrapped his mouth.

"Start singing," she shouted.

"Are you going to wrap my tongue around my mouth again?" said Coyote.

"Just sing," said Old Woman.

So Coyote started to sing again.

"EYOOOOOOOOOW, AWOUUUUUUUUU!"

And as soon as Moon heard Coyote start to sing, she turned around and headed back up into the sky.

"Well," said Old Woman, "this is a fine mess."

"I have an idea," said Coyote. "I'll watch

Moon every night, and whenever she tries to sneak back to the pond, I'll sing to her."

"Oh, no," said all the animals.

"Oh, no," said Old Woman.

But it was the only way to keep Moon in the sky.

So every evening, when Old Woman walked down to the pond to watch Moon come up, Coyote sat on a hill and waited. He combed his fur, ran his tongue around his teeth and wiped his nose on his arm.

"Awooooooooooooooooooo," he sang softly to himself, just to stay in good voice. "Awwwwooooooooooooo."

COYOTE'S NEW SUIT

For Emily, wherever
I may find her — TK

A long time ago when animals and human beings still talked to each other, Coyote had a wonderful suit that he wore everywhere he went.

Each morning Coyote would walk down to the pond.

"Look at my fine suit," Coyote told everyone he saw, stopping only to hug himself and blow kisses at his reflection in the water. "Isn't it the finest suit you've ever seen? I must be the best-dressed creature in the entire world."

One day, when Coyote got to the pond, he found Raven sitting on a branch.

"Good morning," he said. "What are you doing here?"

"Oh, I thought I'd come by to see if anyone needed my help," said Raven.

"As a matter of fact," said Coyote, "you could be very helpful. What do you think of my suit? Isn't it the most excellent suit you've ever seen?"

Raven flapped her wings and stretched her neck.

"It's okay, I guess," she said.

"Okay?" said Coyote. "It is certainly more than okay."

"Actually," said Raven, "it's pretty ordinary. And tan isn't a very exciting color."

"It's not ordinary," said Coyote, "and it's not tan! It's golden, toasty brown."

Raven fluffed her feathers and yawned.

"Feel how soft it is," Coyote continued. "Watch how it shimmers in the light when I dance." And Coyote danced a little, so Raven could see what a truly marvelous suit it was.

Just then, Bear came out of the woods, all hot and sweaty. She took off her bear suit, folded it up neatly and left it on a large flat rock.

"Wheeeeeee!" she shouted, as she hopped

into the pond. She waved her arms and kicked her legs and splashed water all over the place.

"Now that's a suit," said Raven, eyeing Bear's suit as it lay on the rock. "I don't believe I've seen a suit like that in my entire life." And she flew away.

But she didn't go far.

"Hummmph!" grumped Coyote. "What does Raven know about fashion?"

But he had to admit that Bear's suit did look substantial. When no one was looking, he tiptoed over and held the suit up to the light, rubbing his nose in the thick fur.

"It's not as classy as my suit, but it certainly is impressive."

Then Coyote had an idea. It wasn't a good idea, but then most of Coyote's ideas weren't.

"Perhaps," thought Coyote, "I should borrow this suit for a while. Then I can see whether classy or impressive suits me better."

So, while Bear was shampooing her hair

and wiggling her toes and blowing bubbles in the water, Coyote piled her suit onto his shoulders and carried it home.

And no one saw him do this — no one except Raven.

When Bear came out of the water, her suit was gone.

"What happened to my suit?" she asked, looking around. "It was right here a minute ago."

Raven hopped along the branch until she was next to Bear.

"Hello," said Raven. "You're looking a little bare."

Bear was quite grumpy and in no mood for jokes.

"Someone has stolen my suit," she said.

"Really," exclaimed Raven. "I can't imagine who would do such a thing."

"What am I going to do?" asked Bear. "I can't walk around the woods in my underwear."

"Perhaps I can help," said Raven. "Have

you heard about the free clothes at the edge of the woods?"

"Free clothes?" said Bear.

"Oh, yes," said Raven. "Coyote told me about a camp of human beings at the edge of the woods who hang clothes they no longer need on ropes near their houses."

"Clothes they no longer need?" said Bear.

"And anyone who needs clothes can help themselves."

"I never knew human beings were so generous," said Bear.

"But don't let them see you," warned Raven. "Coyote says the human beings have strange ways. They are very shy, and they don't want to know who takes their clothes."

"That was certainly helpful," said Bear, as she hurried off through the woods to find the camp.

"This could be a lot of fun," thought Raven.

When Bear reached the camp, she saw a rope tied between two trees. And hanging from the rope were all sorts of clothes.

"Oh dear," said Bear, as she tried to squeeze into a floral tank top and a pair of gold-foil

pedal pushers. "How can human beings stand to wear such things?"

•

When Coyote got home, he tried on Bear's suit. It was a little too large and a little too heavy, and when Coyote tried to walk, it made him trip.

"It's not exactly my size," he said, as he picked himself up off the floor. "But I certainly look stunning."

Coyote wore Bear's suit to the supermarket. He wore it to the baseball game. He wore it to bingo. And then he hung the suit in his closet and forgot about it.

"The only thing better than having one wonderful suit," said Coyote, "is having two."

The next day Coyote went down to the pond to lie on a rock and admire himself. When he got there, he saw Porcupine swimming laps. And there on a log, neatly folded up, was Porcupine's suit.

"Hmmmmm," said Coyote, touching the ends of the quills. "It's not classy and it's not impressive, but it is quite sporty — and everybody needs a sporty suit from time to time." And Coyote gathered up Porcupine's suit and scampered home.

When Porcupine finished swimming laps and came back to the log to do some stretching exercises, he noticed that his suit was missing. He looked on all the logs. He looked under all the rocks. But he couldn't find his suit anywhere.

"Hey!" shouted Porcupine. "Who took my suit?"

"Did you lose something?" asked Raven, who had seen everything.

"Someone took my suit," said Porcupine.

"Dear me," said Raven. "Who could have done such a thing?"

"This will never do," said Porcupine, pulling his underwear up around his chest as far as he could. "I can't walk around like this."

"Maybe I can help," said Raven. "Just the

other day, Coyote told me something very interesting." And Raven told Porcupine about the camp at the edge of the woods and the human beings who liked to give away their clothes.

"Really?" said Porcupine.

"Just don't let them see you," said Raven. "They are a little strange and very shy, and they don't want to know who takes their clothes."

"Thanks," said Porcupine, as he ran to the

edge of the forest. There, hanging on a rope between two trees, were all sorts of clothes.

"These clothes are awful!" Porcupine said, as he wiggled into a pair of bright yellow pajamas with blue bananas. "No wonder human beings give them away."

•

Porcupine's suit was a little small for Coyote. He had to suck in his stomach and pull in his shoulders and hold his breath just to get it on.

"Lovely," he said, as he admired himself in the mirror. "Look at those quills. I can wear this to all the sporty places."

Coyote wore Porcupine's suit to the supermarket. He wore it to the baseball game. He wore it to bingo. And then he hung it in his closet and forgot about it.

"The only thing better than having two wonderful suits," said Coyote, "is having three."

The next day, Coyote got to the pond just in time to see Skunk and Raccoon and Beaver and Moose playing water polo. And folded up neatly on a large stump were their suits.

"Oh, happy day," cried Coyote, and while Skunk and Raccoon and Beaver and Moose were chasing the ball around the pond, he scooped up their suits and raced home.

When Skunk and Raccoon and Beaver and Moose finished their game and climbed out of the water, they were surprised to find that their suits were no longer on the stump.

"What happened to our suits?" asked Skunk.

"They were right here," said Raccoon.

Raven fluttered out of the tree.

"Is there a problem?" she asked.

"Someone has stolen our clothes," Beaver explained.

"And all we have left is our underwear," said Moose.

"I think I might be able to help," said Raven. And she told Skunk and Raccoon

and Beaver and Moose all about the human beings and the camp at the edge of the woods and the free clothes hanging on the line.

"Just don't let them see you," she warned.

Skunk and Raccoon and Beaver and Moose ran through the woods and crept to the edge of the camp. When no one was looking, they tippy-toed to the clothesline.

"Yaagggh," said Skunk. "I think I'd rather be naked."

"Me, too," said Raccoon.

"Me, too," said Beaver.

"Me, too," said Moose.

•

In the meantime, Coyote was at home trying on his new suits.

"This one is perfect for formal occasions," he said, trying on Skunk's suit.

"The mask is terribly chic," he said, wiggling into Raccoon's suit.

"Leather is always in fashion," he said, adjusting the tail on Beaver's suit.

"Perfect," he said, wrapping Moose's large suit around himself several times. "Just the thing for lounging around after a hard day's work."

Coyote wore his new suits to the supermarket. He wore them to the baseball game. He wore them to bingo. Then he hung them in his closet and forgot about them.

One day, Coyote came home from the pond with Chipmunk's suit.

"It doesn't really fit, but it certainly is lovely," said Coyote, forcing his arm into the

sleeve. "And one can never have too many suits."

But when Coyote went to hang his new suit in the closet, he discovered that there was absolutely no more room.

"Oh dear," he said. "Now what will I do?"

"Perhaps I can be of some help," said Raven, who just happened to be in a nearby tree.

"Why would you help me?" asked Coyote suspiciously.

"Because I'm your friend," said Raven, smiling as sweetly as she could.

"You are?" said Coyote, scratching his head.

"Certainly," said Raven. "Why don't you have a yard sale and sell all of your old suits."

"What an interesting idea," said Coyote. "Why didn't I think of that?"

"You get things ready," said Raven, "and I'll tell everyone about your marvelous sale."

Raven flew to the camp at the edge of the woods. When she arrived, the human beings were all running around in their underwear.

"Goodness," said Raven. "Is this what human beings wear?"

"Certainly not," said the human beings. "Every time we wash our clothes and hang them on the line, someone comes along and steals them."

"Are you in luck!" exclaimed Raven. "Coyote is having a yard sale and he just happens to have an excellent selection of clothing."

"Well, we certainly can't keep running around in our underwear," said the human beings. "Let's go see Coyote."

And while the human beings headed off to Coyote's yard sale, Raven flew back to the woods to find the animals. They were gathered by the pond in their human-being clothes, looking very grumpy.

"What do you want?" they growled.

"I just came by to tell you that Coyote is having a yard sale," said Raven. "And he has a great many fine suits to sell."

"Suits?" asked the animals.

"Oh, yes," said Raven. "I'm sure you'll find everything you need."

"Let's go," said the animals. "These human-being clothes are driving us crazy."

As the animals set off for the sale, Raven quickly flew back to Coyote's house.

"Very impressive," she said, as she watched Coyote hang suits on trees, lay them over stumps and stack them on rocks.

"It's the best suit collection in the entire world," said Coyote, just as the human beings came out of the woods.

"Are these the only clothes you have?" they asked, looking at Coyote's collection.

"A suit for every occasion," said Coyote, sounding rather pleased with himself.

"But these are all animal suits," said the human beings. "Do you have any human-being clothes?"

"Oh, these suits are much nicer," said Coyote.

"But they smell funny," said the human beings.

Coyote wrinkled his nose — the human beings smelled pretty funny themselves.

"Try them on," he suggested. "I'm sure you'll find them warm and snugly."

So the human beings tried on the animal suits, and while they weren't as comfortable as human-being clothing, everyone had to admit that the suits were soft and luxurious.

But just as the human beings were getting used to their new suits, the animals came into the clearing, dressed in their human-being clothes.

"Oh boy," thought Raven. And she hopped around in circles on a branch. "Here comes the fun!"

"Say," said the animals. "Those suits look very familiar."

"Say," said the human beings. "Those clothes look very familiar."

Everyone moved in for a closer look.

"Hey!" said Moose. "That's my suit!"

"Hey!" said a human being. "That's my dress!"

The animals and the human beings got closer and closer, until they were nose to nose.

"It was the human beings who took our suits!" shouted the animals.

"So it was the animals who took our clothes!" shouted the human beings.

And the human beings and the animals began to grumble and push and step on each other's toes.

"Stay calm," said Raven, as she flew down to a rock and fluffed her feathers. "I'm sure we can settle this in a civilized manner."

"Oh, yes," said Coyote, who was upset with all the grumbling and pushing and stepping on toes. "Let's all listen to Raven. She's very helpful."

"Okay," said the animals and the human beings. "But this better be good."

"First of all," said Raven, "we need to discover exactly who's to blame for this mess."

"Yes," said Coyote. "That's a good idea."

"The human beings are to blame," said the

animals. "They took our suits, and they're wearing them right now."

"The animals are to blame," said the human beings. "We got these suits from Coyote. It was the animals who took our clothes, and they're wearing them right now."

"Coyote said these clothes were free," answered the animals.

"My, my," said Raven. "It sounds to me as though … Coyote is to blame."

"Coyote?" said the human beings.

"Coyote?" said the animals.

"Coyote?" said Coyote, who was trying to remember exactly where he had gotten his fine collection of animal suits.

"Of course, you could just trade clothes and suits," said Raven. "That way everyone will be happy."

"The sooner the better," said the animals.

"I don't know," said the human beings. "These animal suits are lovely and warm. And after a while, you get used to the smell."

"We want our suits back," said the animals.

"These suits would be very nice in the winter," said the human beings. "And we're not sure we want to give them back."

"Stop! Stop!" cried Coyote. "All this arguing is going to mess up the world."

"Mind your own business!" shouted the animals.

"Mind your own business!" shouted the human beings.

The animals and the human beings went back to grumbling and shoving and stepping on each other's toes until they were too tired to grumble or shove or step on each other's toes anymore.

"We didn't really want these anyway," said the human beings, and they threw the animal suits on the ground. "They're much too hairy and smelly."

"Well, we certainly don't want these," said the animals, and they threw the human-being clothes on the ground. "They're much too tight and silly-looking."

And before Coyote could say anything, the

animals and the human beings gathered up their suits and their clothes and stomped off.

"This is the last time we talk to you," shouted the human beings, as they marched back to their camp.

"That's just fine with us," shouted the animals, as they headed back to the woods.

•

After everyone had left, Coyote and Raven went down to the pond to relax.

"Thank goodness that's over," said Coyote. "All that arguing was giving me a headache."

"It was certainly exciting," said Raven. "I don't believe I've ever been to a more exciting yard sale."

"I don't know what all the fuss was about," said Coyote. "None of those suits is as wonderful as mine."

"It's okay, I guess," said Raven. "But tan is not a very exciting color."

"It's not tan," said Coyote, looking fondly at his reflection. "It's golden, toasty brown."

Just then, Bear came out of the woods, took off her suit and jumped into the water.

"Now that's a suit," said Raven. "I don't believe I've ever seen a suit like that in my entire life."

"You think so?" asked Coyote. He tiptoed over to Bear's suit and held it up to the light.

"Absolutely," said Raven.

"It's not as classy as my suit," said Coyote, as he rubbed his nose in the thick fur. "But it certainly is impressive."

"Let me know when you have your next yard sale," said Raven, and she flew away.

But she didn't go far.

In case someone needed her help.